Dr. Drabble's Remarkable Underwater Breathing Pills

DR. DRABBLE, GENIUS INVENTOR

Dr. Drabble's Remarkable Underwater Breathing Pills
Dr. Drabble's Spectacular Shrinker-Enlarger
Dr. Drabble and the Dynamic Duplicator

ISBN: 0-8499-3659-4

Printed in the United States of America
94 95 96 97 98 99 LBM 9 8 7 6 5 4 3 2 1

DR.DRABBLE'S
REMARKABLE UNDERWATER
BREATHING PILLS

Written by
Sigmund Brouwer and Wayne Davidson
Illustrated by
Bill Bell

WORD PUBLISHING
Dallas·London·Vancouver·Melbourne

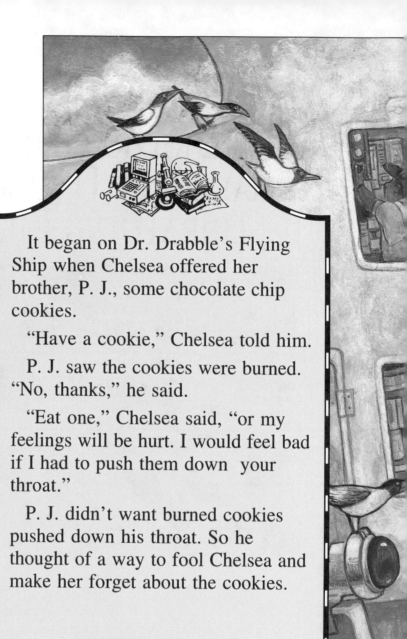

With love,
to Karen, Courtney,
and Chelsea

It began on Dr. Drabble's Flying Ship when Chelsea offered her brother, P. J., some chocolate chip cookies.

"Have a cookie," Chelsea told him.

P. J. saw the cookies were burned. "No, thanks," he said.

"Eat one," Chelsea said, "or my feelings will be hurt. I would feel bad if I had to push them down your throat."

P. J. didn't want burned cookies pushed down his throat. So he thought of a way to fool Chelsea and make her forget about the cookies.

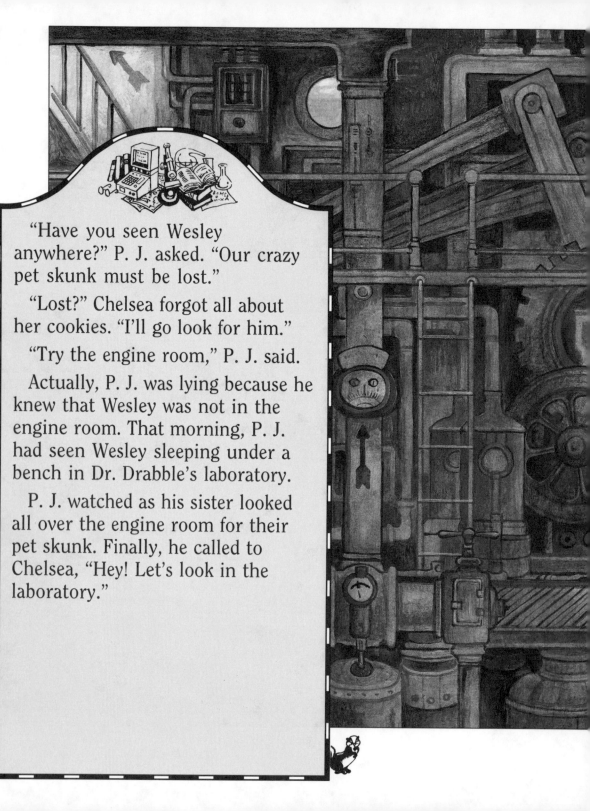

"Have you seen Wesley anywhere?" P. J. asked. "Our crazy pet skunk must be lost."

"Lost?" Chelsea forgot all about her cookies. "I'll go look for him."

"Try the engine room," P. J. said.

Actually, P. J. was lying because he knew that Wesley was not in the engine room. That morning, P. J. had seen Wesley sleeping under a bench in Dr. Drabble's laboratory.

P. J. watched as his sister looked all over the engine room for their pet skunk. Finally, he called to Chelsea, "Hey! Let's look in the laboratory."

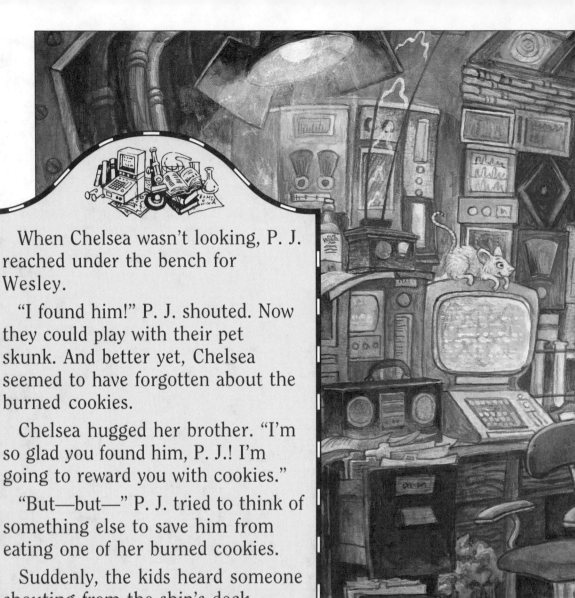

When Chelsea wasn't looking, P. J. reached under the bench for Wesley.

"I found him!" P. J. shouted. Now they could play with their pet skunk. And better yet, Chelsea seemed to have forgotten about the burned cookies.

Chelsea hugged her brother. "I'm so glad you found him, P. J.! I'm going to reward you with cookies."

"But—but—" P. J. tried to think of something else to save him from eating one of her burned cookies.

Suddenly, the kids heard someone shouting from the ship's deck.

It was Arnie Clodbuckle. He didn't like it when Dr. Drabble tried to push him into the ocean.

"No!" Arnie cried. "I can't swim!"

"You're my assistant," Dr. Drabble said. "You have to try out my new invention."

"What new invention?" Chelsea and P. J. asked.

"Remarkable Underwater Breathing Pills," Dr. Drabble said. "They let you breathe underwater and talk to fish."

"We'll try them!" P. J. offered.

"Can we take Wesley, too?" Chelsea asked.

"Okay, you may go. But promise not to go into the deep water," Dr. Drabble said.

Soon they were having a great time swimming near the ship. The reefs around them were filled with all kinds of fish.

"Look at that big rainbow-colored fish!" Chelsea shouted to P. J.

The fish heard Chelsea's shouting. "You are the ugliest fish I ever saw," the grumpy fish said to Chelsea in a grumpy voice. "Go away and take that other ugly fish with you."

"Fish?" Chelsea said. "We're not fish. We're kids. Are you blind? Do you need glasses?"

"Glasses?" the fish asked. "What are glasses?"

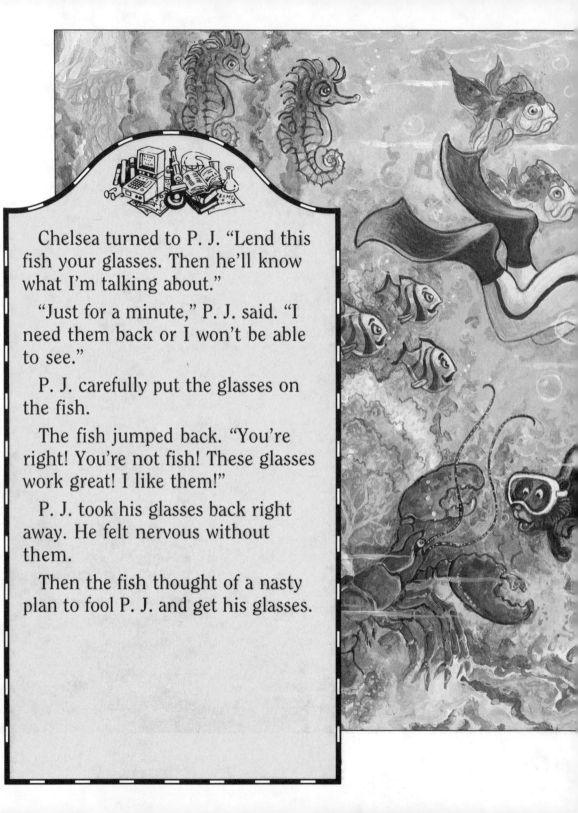

Chelsea turned to P. J. "Lend this fish your glasses. Then he'll know what I'm talking about."

"Just for a minute," P. J. said. "I need them back or I won't be able to see."

P. J. carefully put the glasses on the fish.

The fish jumped back. "You're right! You're not fish! These glasses work great! I like them!"

P. J. took his glasses back right away. He felt nervous without them.

Then the fish thought of a nasty plan to fool P. J. and get his glasses.

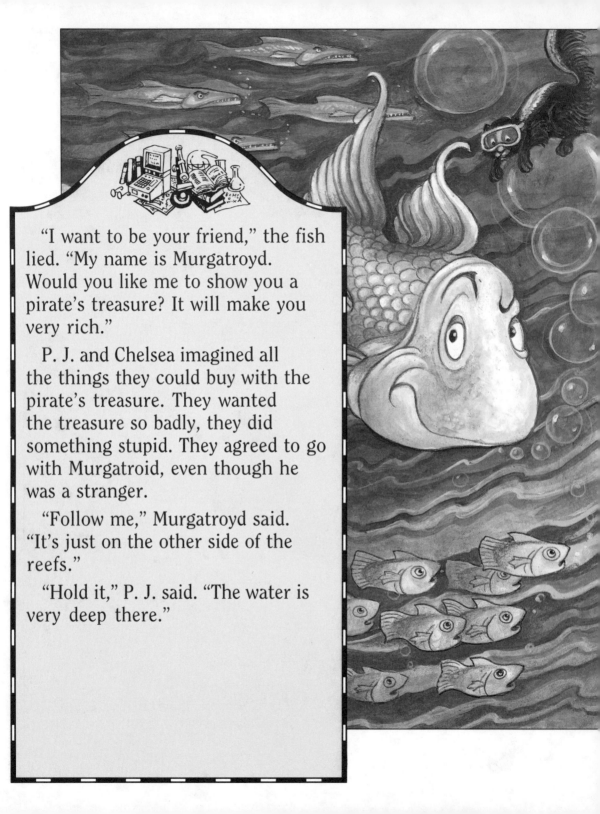

"I want to be your friend," the fish lied. "My name is Murgatroyd. Would you like me to show you a pirate's treasure? It will make you very rich."

P. J. and Chelsea imagined all the things they could buy with the pirate's treasure. They wanted the treasure so badly, they did something stupid. They agreed to go with Murgatroid, even though he was a stranger.

"Follow me," Murgatroyd said. "It's just on the other side of the reefs."

"Hold it," P. J. said. "The water is very deep there."

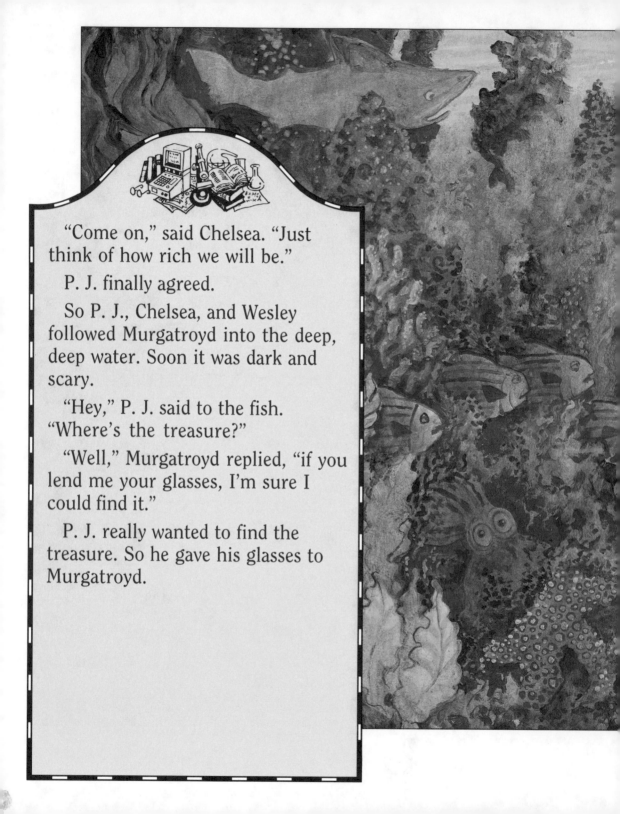

"Come on," said Chelsea. "Just think of how rich we will be."

P. J. finally agreed.

So P. J., Chelsea, and Wesley followed Murgatroyd into the deep, deep water. Soon it was dark and scary.

"Hey," P. J. said to the fish. "Where's the treasure?"

"Well," Murgatroyd replied, "if you lend me your glasses, I'm sure I could find it."

P. J. really wanted to find the treasure. So he gave his glasses to Murgatroyd.

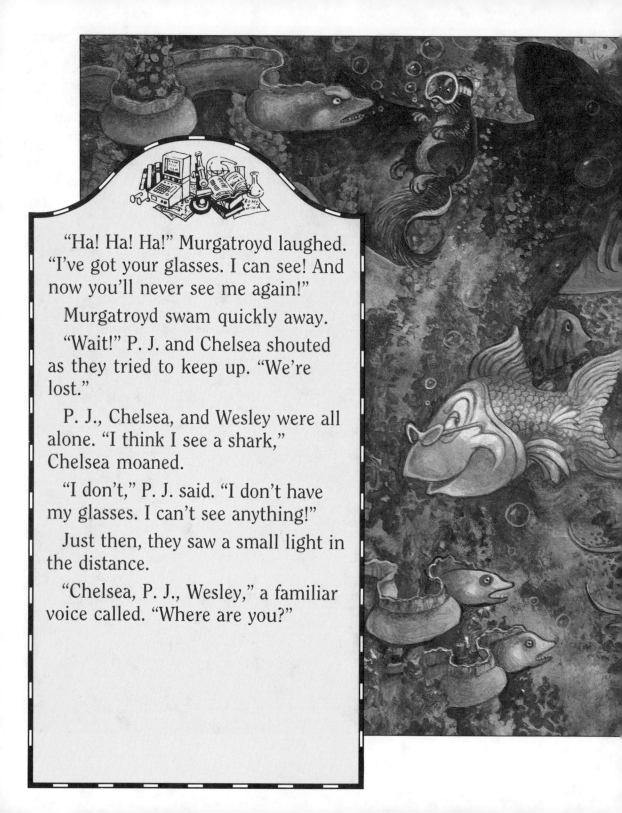

"Ha! Ha! Ha!" Murgatroyd laughed. "I've got your glasses. I can see! And now you'll never see me again!"

Murgatroyd swam quickly away.

"Wait!" P. J. and Chelsea shouted as they tried to keep up. "We're lost."

P. J., Chelsea, and Wesley were all alone. "I think I see a shark," Chelsea moaned.

"I don't," P. J. said. "I don't have my glasses. I can't see anything!"

Just then, they saw a small light in the distance.

"Chelsea, P. J., Wesley," a familiar voice called. "Where are you?"

"Dad!" P. J. and Chelsea shouted and waved.

"I am glad I finally found you," Dad said. "Dr. Drabble forgot to tell you that the Remarkable Underwater Breathing Pills only last a half hour."

Back on the ship, Dad asked, "Why were you in the deep water? And where are your glasses, P. J.?"

P. J. and Chelsea explained how Mugatroyd had lied and tricked them.

Then P. J. said, "Chelsea, I lied to you this morning. I was trying to fool you so I wouldn't have to eat burned cookies. I'm really sorry."

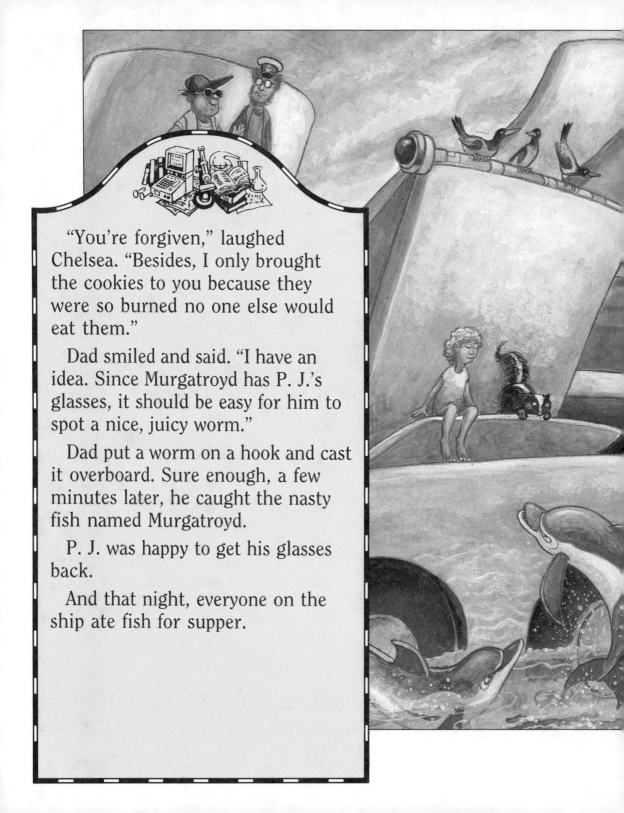

"You're forgiven," laughed Chelsea. "Besides, I only brought the cookies to you because they were so burned no one else would eat them."

Dad smiled and said. "I have an idea. Since Murgatroyd has P. J.'s glasses, it should be easy for him to spot a nice, juicy worm."

Dad put a worm on a hook and cast it overboard. Sure enough, a few minutes later, he caught the nasty fish named Murgatroyd.

P. J. was happy to get his glasses back.

And that night, everyone on the ship ate fish for supper.